The Good

Sheriff's horse

A STORYQUEST BOOK BY

BECCI MURRAY

STORY QUEST

CHOOSE THE PAGE - UNLOCK THE ADVENTURE

ISBN: 978-1-9162069-4-6

Published by Llama House Children's Books

* THE GOOD, THE BAD AND THE SHERIFF'S HORSE IS AN **EXPERT LEVEL** STORYQUEST ADVENTURE *

Welcome to your StoryQuest challenge, the book where YOU are in charge of what happens and YOU are the star of the adventure.

Start your quest on the first page, where your challenge will be explained. At the end of each chapter you'll find two options – choose a page to decide what you want to do next.

As a bonus feature, every StoryQuest book has a SPECIAL CHARACTER hidden amongst the pages. Find the character, and they'll give you a STORYQUEST STAR. This will help you unlock the ultimate ending to your adventure.

There are SO many different paths and SO many different endings – some are good, some are bad, some are happy, some are sad. Which will you choose? Will you complete the challenge? And where will your story end?

Good luck, intrepid StoryQuester, and happy reading!

Shovelling horse poo for pocket money sure does stink. It's worse than wiping tables at the ol' saloon. It's worse than bending horseshoes for the local blacksmith. It's even worse than untangling rope at Lassos 'R' Us.

But this is the Wild West, this is the Sheriff's horse poo and being a stablehand sure beats working for a rustler or a bandit. Here comes the Sheriff now on his horse. He's practising his riding skills for this evening's rodeo.

"Howdy, Sheriff!" you call from the stable.

"Howdy, partner!" smiles the Sheriff, with a wave of his hat. "Mighty fine day for a rodeo, and ain't that the truth. Yee-haw!"

Lightning Bolt is a very skilled horse. Cowgirls and boys come from all over the Wild West to watch him compete in the barrel-race at the annual Maintown Rodeo. And he always, *always* wins.

But this morning, as Lightning Bolt enters the paddock, you notice he's walking a little strangely. He's wriggling like a prairie-dog with fleas, he's squirming like a snake on the hot desert sand, he's kicking his legs like a bucking bronco, and although the Sheriff tries to hold on, he's thrown from his saddle

1

with a loud, "Yee-haaAAAAAARGH!" where he lands in the big pile of poo you just shovelled out of the stable.

SPLAT!

"Sheriff!" you cry, running to pull him out. "What's wrong with your horse?"

The man sighs as he wipes the poo from his eye.

"We giddy-upped into a cactus out west," he replies. "Lightnin' Bolt prickled his bee-hind and caught the Itchity Fever. He'll be all tickly-scratchy for weeks."

"But it's the rodeo tonight," you remind him. "Everyone will be so disappointed if you don't compete. What are you going to do?"

"Ain't much I *can* do," sighs the Sheriff. "Course, my Great Grandpappy Pete woulda cured him in no time. He was a medicine man and he had a recipe for an Itchity Fever medicine. But I can't go skedaddlin' all over the Wild West lookin' for ingredients – not when there's a rodeo to set up." The Sheriff pauses. His eyes sparkle and the corners of his moustache twitch. "I don't suppose *you* could look for 'em instead?"

"*Me?!*" you gasp. "But, Sheriff, travelling out of town isn't safe. The Wild West is ruled by thieves and bandits, not to mention all those snakes and jackals and goats I'd run into." (Yes, even the *goats* of the Wild

West are dangerous.) You sigh heavily. "Although, I suppose anything's better than shovelling poo. I'll do it!"

"Yee-haw!" cheers the Sheriff. "Thanks, kid! There are three ingredients you'll need to find: a pint of buffalo milk, a fresh dragon fruit, and the feather of a Four-Legged Duck."

(Sorry, did he just say, *the feather of a Four-Legged Duck?*)

The Sheriff whistles and a scruffy mule ambles in from a neighbouring field.

"You can borrow my ol' pal Tumbleweed to speed up your journey. There's hay in her saddlebag but eatin' it makes her windier than a desert typhoon – you'll do well to remember that. And don't go losin' her, or you won't make it back in time for the rodeo."

"Don't lose the mule," you repeat. "Got it."

The Sheriff takes a book out of his pocket.

"This notebook belonged to my Great Grandpappy Pete. He drew pictures of the all ingredients he used in his medicines and a map of the Wild West to help him find 'em. You can take it with you. And here are some coins and my divination stick too." You put the items into your saddlebag and the Sheriff raises a bushy eyebrow. "So, are you ready for your StoryQuest to begin?"

A surge of determination shoots from the soles of your boots to the top of your hat.

"Yee-haw!" you cry. "I'm ready, Sheriff!"

"Then saddle-up, partner, and remember – *do not lose the mule* or you won't make it back in time for the rodeo," and with that, you head out onto the perilous plains of the Wild West on a quest to save the Sheriff's horse.

Your StoryQuest has begun! Turn to page 49.

You take the divination stick out of your saddlebag in the hope of finding water. It looks like a large twig with a forked end. You've no idea how it works, so you hold it up in the air and watch it carefully, as Tumbleweed trots to the northernmost side of the desert.

"This is ridiculous," you mutter, more than an hour later. "How on earth can a *stick* tell us where to find water? I mean, I've heard some tall stories in my time, but I've never heard anything sillier than a twig that can find—"

SPLASH!

You were so busy looking up at the divination stick, you didn't notice Blue River right there in front of you. It's definitely *wet* enough here for ducks, but there are none in sight. So you wade across to the other side and climb onto the bank, where Tumbleweed shakes herself like a wet dog.

In front of you lies a dense forest known as Green Woodland. It's as good a place as any to search for a Four-Legged Duck, so you venture into the trees.

Before long, you come across a make-shift tent; a big sheet of canvas thrown over a low branch. A scruffy-looking man crawls out. He has a full beard, shoulder-length hair and eyebrows you could tie knots in.

At first you think he's a yeti, but then you decide he must be a hermit. Do you want to talk to him about Four-Legged Ducks?

Yes, please – he looks like an intelligent sort of chap.
Turn to page 71.
No, thank you – he looks proper scary. Turn to page 98.

You lean right and the raft drifts east, where the river carries you through the great fir trees of Green Woodland. You can hear the birds singing and feel the gentle rocking of the water, and you think to yourself, "Ah yes, StoryQuesting is the life for me."

But there's a bend in the river. And suddenly you're thrown into a long stretch of white-water rapids, where you're tossed around by the raging current like a stone in a cowboy's boot.

You cling to the raft with both hands, but Tumbleweed can't keep her footing. Your mule's about to fall into the water – you'll need to do something and fast!

To shout for help, turn to page 46.
To throw Tumbleweed to safety, turn to page 57.

The summit of Purple Mountain is too steep for a mule, so you tie Tumbleweed to a tree as you start the difficult climb.

Wow, the air's thin up here! But you move fast and eventually reach the summit. From here, you have a breath-taking view of the Wild West. You can see Crabbity Jack's Shack below you and Blue River running alongside it, then beyond that the arid Wilderness with Maintown at its centre.

Now you know *exactly* how to get home!

Yee-haw!

Hurriedly, you scramble down the rocky slope and run to the tree where you left your mule. But Tumbleweed isn't there! Someone must have untied her! And as you scan the side of the mountain, a terrible sound fills the air.

MEHHHHHHHHHHHHH!

You turn suddenly and find yourself face to face with the scariest, rottenest, grisliest band of villains in the whole of the Wild West. *Goats!* A huge heard of them! They've chewed through Tumbleweed's reins and they're holding her captive in the trunk of a hollowed-out sycamore tree.

You're terrified (and who wouldn't be?), but

you've come too far to give up and no wonky-toothed farmyard bandits are going to stand between you and that mule.

Bravely, you march towards the tree stump with your head held high. The goats circle around you, scuffing the ground and chewing the air with menace. When you duck inside the hollowed trunk, they think you're surrendering to their supreme goatiness. But then you snatch a handful of hay out of Tumbleweed's saddlebag and the herd panics.

Their eyes bulge like gobstoppers and the biggest goat makes a dash for the tree, so you quickly feed Tumbleweed the hay, take hold of her saddle and…

PAAAARRRRRRRRRRRRP!

The mule's windy bottom sends the pair of you shooting out of the trunk like a big, furry cannonball, scattering goats in every direction as you whiz down the side of Purple Mountain, across Blue River, through the Wilderness and into the centre of Maintown, where you land in a crumpled heap in the Sheriff's stable.

Wow, that was some mule-ride, partner!

With no time to lose before the rodeo starts, you grab the mucking-out bucket and pour in the buffalo milk. Then you squeeze in the juice from the fresh dragon fruit and drop the beautifully striped feather into the mix.

At once, something wonderful happens. Little multicoloured bubbles rise to the surface of the mixture. They float up out of the bucket and then burst into tiny rainbows, each one falling back into the medicine like blossom as the feather crumbles into a sparkling, golden dust.

Your Itchity Fever medicine is ready! Yee-haw!

Hurriedly, you run outside to the paddock with your bucket. Lightning Bolt is itching himself on a tree, but with a little encouragement you persuade him to taste the mixture. He likes it. In fact, he likes it *so* much that he drinks the whole bucketful and burps out the biggest rainbow you've ever seen.

BAAAAAAAAAAAAAARP!

A beautiful arc of colours stretches out across the Wild West and the Sheriff's horse stops wriggling.

You've cured Lightning Bolt of his Itchity Fever and are the most magnificent StoryQuester that ever lived! But will you tell the Sheriff your good news *before the rodeo*, or surprise him at the barrel-race?

To tell the Sheriff before the rodeo, turn to page 82.
To take Lightning-Bolt straight to the rodeo as a surprise, turn to page 36.

Great Grandpappy Pete's Drawings of Medicinal Feathers

The feather of a Long-Nosed Peacock is good for patients who are being sat on by a horse. A doctor should use the feather to tickle the animal under its armpit or on the foot. This will make the horse giggle so much it will fall off the patient. Please note, finding the armpit of an animal without arms can often prove tricky.

The feather of a Sabre-Toothed Robin is an excellent treatment for patients who are stuck in the swing-door of a saloon. The medically trained person should drop the feather near the patient, shouting, "Argh! A Sabre-Toothed Robin! We're all goners!" and the patient will immediately unstick themselves from the door and run off down the street.

The feather of a Four-Legged Duck is known for its use on patients who prickle themselves on a cactus. It can be mixed with a pint of buffalo milk and the juice of a fresh dragon fruit and used as an effective cure for Itchity Fever.

You've learnt what the feather of a Four-Legged Duck looks like! Turn to page 41 to continue your quest.

You go to the local store to buy a new bowl. The bell goes *TING!* as you open the door and a middle-aged woman stands up behind the counter.

"Howdy," she smiles. Her messy hair and prickly chin remind you of a cactus. "I'm Mrs Bullwinkle. Welcome to Maintown Store. What can I get you?"

"I'd like to buy a mixing bowl, please," you reply.

Mrs Bullwinkle lifts a ceramic pot down from one of the shelves and places it onto the counter.

"You're lucky," she says, as you pick up the bowl. "It's my last one. That'll be two gold coins, please."

But you don't have any coins. You used them all getting into the rodeo.

"Erm, would you mind if I paid you later, please?" you ask sheepishly, your face going a little red.

"Yes, I do mind!" snaps the storekeeper. "If you ain't got no money, you can get outta my store. Go on, clear off!"

Mrs Bullwinkle makes a grab for the bowl.

Instinctively, you pull it away.

And…

CRASH!

It slips out of your hands and smashes all over the floor.

Mrs Bullwinkle is furious. Her prickly chin turns red and bristly, as she runs out from behind the counter and locks the door. She won't let you out of her store until you've pieced the whole thing back together again, by which time the rodeo will have finished.

Well, ain't that a pain in the neckerchief?

Bad luck, partner.

Go back to the start of the book to try again, or turn to page 66 to make a different choice.

You trot down the crumbling slopes of Dead Man's Gorge, fanning yourself with your hat. It's even hotter here than it was in the Wilderness. This side of Grey Rock catches the most sunlight at this time of day and the heat is unbearable.

The mule's feet are already starting to drag.

She might get sunstroke if you don't take shelter.

To the east of Dead Man's Gorge is a disused gold mine. It's a large stone building with broken windows and no door. You could go inside to get out of the sun, but it's kind of spooky-looking and you can already see Ancient Annie's Buffalo Farm in the distance.

Will you carry on, or take shelter in the old mine?

To shelter in the old mine, turn to page 90.
To carry on until you reach Ancient Annie's Buffalo Farm, turn to page 53.

As your windy mule lands back on her feet, you head south into the Wilderness, where the landscape is bare and dry. Leafless plants cling to life, snakes hunt on the dusty ground and a faint breeze ruffles your hair, as you ride through the nothingness.

In the near distance, you see a man on horseback. He has a neckerchief pulled over his face and a hat down to his eyebrows. The rider skids to a halt in front of you.

"Gimme your money!" he growls. "And your donkey too!"

"She's not a donkey," you tell him. "She's a mule. And you can't have her, I'm afraid. You see, I'm on a quest to cure the Sheriff's horse."

The man snatches the neckerchief down from his face. He has a scar on his cheek and half his teeth are missing.

"Look, kid, don't you know who I am?" You shrug. You have no idea who he is. You've never been out of Maintown until today. "I'm Billy the Goat, the meanest, baddest, rottenest bandit in the whole of the Wild West. Yee-haw!"

Uh oh. Bandits are dangerous.

You'd better be nice to him.

"Pleased to meet you, Billy the Goat," you reply, a little *too* nicely perhaps. "I don't know your face, but I *do* know your name. You're a very successful bandit, Billy the Goat."

The man sighs.

"I used to be," he replies. "But life's tough out here in the Wilderness. I'm doin' my best to steal an honest livin', but it ain't all ruby rings and gold nuggets. Folk ain't got much to take these days. I mean, look at you, trottin' around the Wild West on the back of a donkey."

"I'm sorry life's hard for you right now, Billy the Goat," you reply. "But if being a bandit is so difficult, why don't you get a job?"

Something lights up in his face. It's as if the idea of getting a job has never occurred to him before.

"A...*job*," muses Billy the Goat, like he's saying the word for the very first time. "Now, there's a thought. But who's gonna hire an ex-bandit?"

"I know the Sheriff of Maintown," you say. "If you tell him I sent you, I'm sure he'll find you something."

The bandit sniffs. Then he takes off his neckerchief to blow his nose.

"Why, that's the kindest thing anyone's ever said to me," he sobs. "I'll go to Maintown right away. Now, tell me, kid, what can Billy the Goat do for you in return?"

"Oh, well, I need some buffalo milk. Do you know where I can find some?"

"Sure do," replies Billy the Goat. "Ancient Annie's Buffalo Farm is just over yonder. Keep walking south 'til you get to Grey Rock, then go around it to reach the farm. The eastern side will take you through Snake Valley, the western side goes via Dead Man's Gorge. Good luck, kid, and thanks for the help," and with that, he gallops north towards Maintown.

And so, as Billy the Goat grows small in the distance, you head over to Grey Rock. Snake Valley is to your right and Dead Man's Gorge is to your left. Both sound like places you'd rather avoid, but which route will you take?

To go through Snake Valley, turn to page 92.
To go via Dead Man's Gorge, turn to page 14.

You throw a rock to get Crabbity Jack's attention. The missile flies over the fence, past the man's head and – *SMASH!* – straight through the side of his greenhouse.

Oopsie!

The old man eyes the shattered glass with a furious look, then glowers over his shoulder before marching towards you with his arms swinging low.

"WHADDA YA RECKON YOU'RE PLAYIN' AT?" he shouts, when he gets to the fence.

"I-I'm sorry," you tell him, "I didn't mean to cause any damage. I was trying to attract your attention."

"CRACKED MY EXTENSION? THAT AIN'T NO EXTENSION, YOU FOOL, THAT'S A GREENHOUSE!"

It seems Crabbity Jack is a little hard of hearing.

"No, I said, I was trying to *attract your attention*."

"ATTACK MY INVENTION? WHAT INVENTION?"

"No, *attract…your…attention*."

"YOU AIN'T GONNA EXTRACT NONE O' MY PENSION, YOU CHEEKY YOUNG SCALLYWAG – IT'S *MY* PENSION, NOT YOURS. NOW, GIMME SOME MONEY TO PAY FOR THIS GREENHOUSE."

You have four gold coins in your saddlebag, but they belong to the Sheriff. You're supposed to use them to buy ingredients for the medicine. Should you give them to Crabbity Jack, or explain why he can't have the money?

To give the money to Crabbity Jack, turn to page 44.
To explain why he can't have it, turn to page 68.

You feel a flutter of excitement as you start the long climb to the summit of Purple Mountain. The grassy slopes become rockier the higher up you go and there's a man herding sheep in the distance.

But suddenly, Tumbleweed's legs become wobbly. She's swaying from side to side, staggering up the mountain as if someone just rolled her downhill in an empty barrel.

You climb out of your saddle to investigate.

"There there, old friend," you tell her, patting the top of her furry head, "you'll be all right. Some deep breaths will make you feel better. In through the nose, and out through the mouth, in through the nose, and out through the mouth, in through the nose, and—"

BOOF!

That is the sound of a mule fainting.

You see, the poor creature has been breathing in your terrible stink ever since you left Crabbity Jack's Shack and all those deep breaths have pushed her over the edge. She'll be fine once you've had a wash, but after that you should take her home so she can recover from her ordeal in her nice, comfy, sweet-smelling mule shed.

Never mind, partner. You can use what you've

learnt on your next attempt – just make sure you take a bath first.

Phooey!

Go back to the start of the book to try again, or turn to page 56 to make a different choice.

Wow, your mountain lion impressions are incredible! The jackal is terrified, especially when you swish your imaginary mane and gnash your fake lion-teeth, and he runs away with his tail between his legs.

But it seems your skills were a little *too* good. For suddenly, from behind the skull of a large wildebeest, an *actual* lion appears. He's mistaken you for a member of his pride and runs over to rescue you from the jackal. Of course, when he finds a human being and a tasty mule instead, he eyes the pair of you like a family-size pizza with extra cheese.

Talk about out of the frying pan and into the fire.

Why won't these animals leave you alone?!

How are you going to escape?

To keep doing your lion impression, turn to page 76.

To run to the nearest cactus patch and hide, turn to page 94.

Tumbleweed carries you quietly through the undergrowth towards the nest. It's well-hidden by a branch, so you climb down and part the leaves. The bird's feathers look like the one in Great Grandpappy Pete's drawing, but she's fast asleep and you can't see her legs.

Carefully, you pick up a twig and use it to lift the bird's tail.

SQUAWK! PECK!

Now, here's the thing about birds.

SQUAWK! PECK!

They don't like being poked at with twigs.

SQUAWK! PECK!

No-one likes being poked at with twigs.

SQUAWK! PECK!

Especially not when they're sleeping.

SQUAWK! PECK!

Especially not when they're sitting on a nest full of eggs.

SQUAWK! PECK!

The bird flaps her wings madly and her eyes turn red. They bulge from their sockets like two bright holly berries as she flies into your face, pecking you on the head through a cloud of feathers.

The attack startles your mule. She bucks her hind legs and the saddlebag slides off her back. It lands in the water then floats to the middle of the lake, where a milky white cloud spreads out on the surface as the bag sinks into the weeds.

The little bird alights on a nearby branch and crows happily, as she dances around on her *two* yellow legs.

Gee, partner, that sure is bad luck.

Go back to the start of the book to try again, or turn to page 103 to make a different choice.

Crabbity Jack's Shack is near Purple Mountain. Its lofty peak can be seen from all over the Wild West, so you head towards it on the back of your mule.

After an hour of riding, you reach the western bank of Blue River. There's a large wooden hut on the opposite side – it must be Crabbity Jack's Shack. Next to it, there's a glass greenhouse and a small chicken coop, beyond which a herd of buffalo are grazing on the lush grass. A rickety fence encircles the land, with a wonky gate and a sign you can't read from this side of the river.

You'll need to cross over the water to see what it says. But how?

To make a raft, turn to page 39.
To swim across, turn to page 54.

"That's very kind," you say, "but I have to get on with my quest."

Ancient Annie sighs glumly.

"I understand," she says. "Let's milk a buffalo so you can be on your way."

The old woman shows you across the farm and into the buffalo shed. The floor is covered with straw and there's a hay-bale in the corner. But where are the buffalo?

As you turn to ask Ancient Annie that very question, the door slams and you find yourself alone in a very dark barn.

"Hey, what's going on?" you cry.

The old woman's eyeball peeps through a knot-hole in the wall.

"I ain't seen no-one in a long time, kid, and I do so like a chat. Now, settle down while I tell you *all* about myself…"

The old woman talks for hours.

And hours.

And *hours*.

By nightfall you know every detail of her one-hundred-and-nine years, including the time she married a shepherd on Purple Mountain and had twelve sheep as bridesmaids.

The rodeo will be over by the time you get out of this shed. But you've made a new friend (albeit a rather scary one) and have all the buffalo milk you could ever wish for.

Go back to the start of the book to try again or turn to page 92 to make a different choice.

"Okay," you tell him, "you can take the four coins."

The shepherd snatches them up with glee.

"Ha!" he laughs, handing you the feather. "You've paid *way* too much! So long, sucker!" and he ushers his flock to the other side of the mountain.

That shepherd is a conman.

He has taken advantage of your good nature.

But you've collected *all three* of your ingredients, so who cares? Yee-haw! All you have to do now is go home and make the Itchity Fever medicine in time for the rodeo.

Hurriedly, you look for Maintown on the distant horizon. But you can't see it. You must be standing on the wrong side of Purple Mountain. How will you find your way home?

If you want to climb to the peak of Purple Mountain for a better view of the land, turn to page 8.
If you want to ask Tumbleweed how to get back to Maintown, turn to page 86.

"Yes, please," you say, "that would be lovely."

You tie Tumbleweed to a tree and go into the wooden farmhouse. Ancient Annie makes a fresh pot of tea and serves you a slice of cake. You tell her all about the Sheriff's horse and she tells you all about the time she was a bare-knuckle fighter in Texas City.

When it's time to get on with your quest, the old lady fetches some fresh buffalo milk from her larder. You thank Ancient Annie then step outside to say your goodbyes, where you realise something awful has happened.

Tumbleweed is missing and so are Annie's buffalo!

In the distance, you see a lone horseman riding south. He's towing Tumbleweed on a small trailer and herding Annie's buffalo away from the farm. It's Billy the Goat! He fooled you into thinking he was going to Maintown and turned his hand to rustling instead.

Ancient Annie is furious. She throws you off her farm and you're forced to walk home through Snake Valley alone. Good luck with those serpents, StoryQuester!

Go back to the start of the book to try again, or turn to page 92 to make a different choice.

The Desert of Bones sounds like the kind of place a StoryQuester should go, so you enter the desolate land on the back of your trusty mule.

Phew, it sure is warm here! It's like walking around in an oven with your winter coat on and a hot-water-bottle shoved up your jumper. Your sweaty pong mixes with the smell of buffalo dung to make one giant stink and Tumbleweed is very unhappy. She doesn't like the smell of sweaty buffalo dung, so she kicks her legs in protest and tosses you out of your saddle, before turning tail and trotting back to Maintown.

You can't finish your quest without her, but you can try the Sheriff's challenge again once you've taken a bath.

Go back to the start of the book to try again, or turn to page 56 to make a different choice.

You lean left and the raft travels west along the river. The water here is littered with logs. They're floating in your path like sleeping crocodiles, so you drift carefully in and out of them, taking care not to damage your raft.

Suddenly, one of the logs lifts its head. Then it opens its mouth and shows you its sharp, pointed teeth. Yikes! They're not logs – they really *are* crocodiles!

SNAP!

The first croc almost catches Tumbleweed's tail.

SNAP!

The second tears a hole in your shirt.

SNAP!

And the third just misses your leg as it bites clean through the middle of the raft, leaving you on one half and the mule on the other.

Tumbleweed's side floats to the riverbank, where the old mule saunters onto the bank and disappears into Green Woodland. But the Blue River current takes hold of your portion and carries you through the crocodiles, past the forest and out onto the ocean itself.

Three days later a passing fishing-boat picks you up and ships you back to Maintown, where the Sheriff is mighty relieved you're safe even though you haven't found any ingredients.

Try again soon, partner, and watch out for those crocs!

Go back to the start of the book to try again, or turn to page 39 make a different choice.

As your windy mule lands back on her feet, you head north into the Wilderness.

Tumbleweed trots merrily over the dusty ground, glad to be out of the mule-shed on this beautiful sunny day, when a stagecoach trundles into view. You could ask its passengers if they know where you can find your ingredients.

Hurriedly, you climb out of your saddle and wave your arms in front of the horses. The driver pulls on the reins and the carriage skids to a halt. A large woman in a brown leather suit jumps out. She storms towards you with fury in her eyes, her thick arms swinging at her sides.

There are bears less scary than this on Purple Mountain.

"Dagnabbit!" yells the woman. "I am so darn sick of you thievin' bandits tryin' to hijack my stagecoach! If you want it, you'll have to get through *me* first, or my name ain't Calamity Joan," and she pushes her sleeves up to show you her hairy fists.

Crikey! Calamity Joan is a well-known frontierswoman in these parts. Even the famous bandit, Billy the Goat, is scared of Calamity Joan.

"I-I'm not a thief," you stammer. "I'm just a

stablehand from Maintown. I'm on a quest to cure the Sheriff's horse. Do you know where I can buy some buffalo milk?"

Calamity Joan lowers her fists, but her eyes are still fixed upon yours.

"You could try Crabbity Jack's Shack," she replies. "Ol' Jack keeps a buffalo herd up near Purple Mountain. It's quite a distance to travel by donkey though."

"Oh, she's not a donkey," you tell her. "She's a mule," and you immediately regret having said that.

Calamity Joan curls her top lip.

"Or," she goes on, "you could try the Wilderness Store. It's just over yonder, but there ain't much call for buffalo milk around these parts, so there mightn't be any in stock. Now, get away from my stagecoach, kid, or it'll be fisty-cuffs at dawn," and she climbs back into her carriage.

Where do you want to go next?

If you'd like to go the distance and head over to Crabbity Jack's Shack, turn to page 25.
If you'd rather go to the Wilderness Store, turn to page 105.

You couldn't care less about cactus plants, so you set off through the desert in search of a fresh dragon fruit.

As you trek across the sandy plains, you become aware of a gentle breeze pushing in from the east. It's a welcome break from the scorching heat of the sun, but as the wind grows stronger, it whips at the ground and the air becomes swamped in a haze of orange.

Yikes! A sandstorm!

Tumbleweed can't see where she's going and all she can do is walk aimlessly on in the hope she will find a way out. But when the sand settles many hours later, the cactus patch is still next to you.

You've been travelling in circles for hours and now you're late for the rodeo. Gee, that sucks.

StoryQuest over. Go back to the start of the book to try again.

You take Lightning Bolt into town to surprise the Sheriff, and what a surprise it is.

"Well, bless my boots!" he exclaims. "You've cured my horse of his Itchity Fever! You truly are the best stablehand a Sheriff could wish for! C'mon, partner, let's saddle-up – the rodeo is about to begin!"

This year's celebrations are the greatest you've ever seen. There are people in fancy-dress, a sheep-herding contest, a ragtime band playing your favourite songs, line-dancing groups, yummy food and the most popular riding contest this side of Blue River – the grand barrel-race.

All the best riders have travelled across the Wild West to compete. They saddle-up and gallop around two barrels, in and out of the obstacles as fast as their horses will carry them, and the quickest time wins. But of course, no-one ever beats the Sheriff and that's all part of the fun.

At the end of the competition, Lightning Bolt is awarded a big rosette and the Sheriff tells everyone about his awesome stablehand, who crossed deserts and climbed mountains to save his trusty stead.

A huge cheer goes up as you and Tumbleweed take your place next to the Sheriff.

"I've been thinking," he says, as the crowd go crazy, "a Wild West explorer like you shouldn't be shovelling horse poo for pocket money – how would you like to be my Deputy instead?"

No more poo-shovelling! Yippee!

And later that evening, as the reddening sun sinks into the distant horizon, you walk Tumbleweed back to her shed with your shiny new Deputy's badge twinkling on your hat.

"Gee," you sigh, as your furry friend settles down for the night, "this sure has been a mighty fine adventure."

The mule releases a little wind, and you're pretty sure what she means by that is…

"Yee-haw!"

Congratulations! You've completed your quest and you're going to be the new Deputy Sheriff of Maintown!
If you want to find the ultimate ending to your story, go back to the start of the book and try your adventure again.

Great Grandpappy Pete's Drawings of Medicinal Cacti

Prickly Pear

A Prickly Pear is the fruit of an Optunia cactus. It is a mighty fine cure for Spikyitis boils. Just rub the fruit onto the patient's skin and their boils will burst open like small volcanoes. Warning: do not eat a Prickly Pear after rubbing it onto your boils - it will not taste good.

A Sword Pear is perfect for patients with Thorn Pox. Simply boil the fruit in a pan with a spoonful of sugar cane, then ask the patient to eat the mixture whilst balancing a small bison on their head. It won't cure anything, but it will take their mind off the pox.

Sword Pear

Strawberry Pear

Strawberry Pears grow on Stenocereus cacti and are also known as dragon fruits. When mixed with buffalo milk and the feather of a Four-Legged Duck they are a good cure for Itchity Fever.

You know where to find a dragon fruit! Yee-haw!

Turn to page 102 to continue your quest.

You gather some sticks to build your raft and lay them out on the riverbank. There's an old lasso in the Sheriff's saddlebag. You use it to tie them together, then push the raft out onto the river.

Tumbleweed steps aboard your makeshift boat. She bobs on the water like a big, hairy duck, then you sit down next to her and let go of the bank.

At once, the current takes hold of your raft and pulls you downstream. You paddle frantically, but the water's heading north and so are you, away from Crabbity Jack's Shack, past the Desert of Bones and on towards Green Woodland.

Cripes, there's a fork in the river!

Lean left to go west, or right to go east!

To lean left, turn to page 31.
To lean right, turn to page 7.

Shovelling buffalo poo is very similar to shovelling horse poo, except buffalos are bigger and so is the shovel. It's hard work, but you're an experienced stablehand and soon your job is complete.

Crabbity Jack comes over to inspect your work.

"WHY, YOU'RE THE BEST DARN POO-SHOVELLER THIS SIDE OF GREEN WOODLAND!" he shouts in your face. It's not the greatest compliment you've ever had, but you'll take it. He hands you a pint of his finest buffalo milk. "I RECKON YOU'VE EARNT THIS, KID!"

Yee-haw! You've found your first ingredient and are an incredible human being, but you smell like an elephant's litter-tray after all that shovelling.

Do you want to clean up your act before you search for the other ingredients?

I stink! I'll take a wash in the river. Turn to page 89.

Washing is for wimps! I'll get on with my quest. Turn to page 56.

"It really *is* a Four-Legged Duck feather!" you tell the shepherd. "Here, I have some money in my saddlebag."

You take out the coins and show them to the man.

"WOW, FOUR GOLD COINS!" he exclaims. "I could buy a whole extra flock of sheep with those. Hand 'em over and the feather's yours."

"What, *all* of them?" you gasp. "Four gold coins is a *lot* of money to pay for a feather."

"But this is a very *rare* feather," the shepherd replies. "So either pay up or look somewhere else."

The shepherd wants all four of the Sheriff's gold coins in exchange for one measly feather. What are you going to do?

To give him the four gold coins, turn to page 28.
To make up a sob-story so he lets you buy the feather for a better price, turn to page 85.

You take the StoryQuest Star out of your saddlebag and hand it to the Sheriff.

"You found it!" he cries, his face lighting up with joy. "That sure is mighty fine news, kid! And because you collected the star, there'll be a surprise for you after the barrel-race. But first, let's skedaddle – the rodeo is about to begin!"

This year's celebrations are the greatest you've ever seen. There are people in fancy-dress, a sheep-herding contest, a ragtime band playing your favourite songs, line-dancing groups, yummy food and the most popular riding contest this side of Blue River – the grand barrel-race.

All the best riders have travelled across the Wild West to compete. They saddle-up and gallop around two barrels, in and out of the obstacles as fast as their horses will carry them, and the quickest time wins. But of course, no-one ever beats the Sheriff and that's all part of the fun.

At the end of the competition, the crowd gathers round for the Sheriff's speech.

"Cowgirls and boys," he begins, "I have an announcement to make – this will be my last rodeo as the Sheriff of Maintown. I've decided it's time to retire."

There's a groan of disappointment, but the Sheriff holds up the StoryQuest Star and the people go silent.

"A Sheriff is brave and honest," he says. "And a Sheriff works hard to find the ultimate end to their story, no matter what obstacles stand in their way. Today I set a test, to see if my young stablehand was up to the challenge, and all I can say is… *Yee-haw, partner, you rock!* Cowgirls and boys, let's hear it for the new Sheriff of Maintown!"

The word **SHERIFF** appears on the StoryQuest Star and a cheer goes up as it's pinned to your hat. Then Tumbleweed is rewarded with a frilly rosette and a huge bag of hay.

"This sure has been a mighty fine Wild West adventure," you tell your four-legged friend, as she chomps down her tasty prize, "but I couldn't have done it without you," and as the blazing sun sinks into the distant horizon, a very happy, very windy mule soars across the reddening skyline.

Yee-haw!

Congratulations! You've found the ultimate ending to your StoryQuest adventure and have become the new Sheriff of Maintown! Gee, partner, you're awesome.

You give Crabbity Jack the Sheriff's money. He looks down at the four coins, then back up at you.

"THIS AIN'T ENOUGH TO FIX MY GREENHOUSE!" he shouts. "YOU'LL HAVE TO WORK ON MY FARM TO MAKE UP THE REST! THERE'S A STABLE BEHIND THE SHACK WITH YOUR NAME ON IT AND A WHOLE LOTTA BUFFALO POO THAT NEEDS SHOVELLIN'!"

Oh no, not *more* poo!

This is going to take you all day!

That evening you return to Maintown with no ingredients and the Sheriff docks your wages until you've paid back all of his coins. But don't worry, StoryQuester – you can use what you've learnt to complete the Sheriff's challenge on your next attempt.

Yee-haw!

Go back to the start of the book to try again, or turn to page 18 to make a different choice.

You run from the alligator and start the long climb to the top of Purple Mountain, imagining all the fearsome creatures who might live on these slopes: eagles the size of dragons, wolves with teeth like daggers and bears with razor-sharp claws. But never in your worst nightmare did you think you would face the hideous beast that now crosses your path.

Its teeth are gruesomely wonky, its ears are repulsively floppy, its tail is horrendously cute and its voice sounds like the call of a startled sheep.

"*MEHHHHHHHHHHHHHHHHHH!*"

Buckle up, partner, you've been seen by a *goat!*

The creature stares at you through bulging eyes (well, through *one* bulging eye – the other one's swivelling around in its socket with a life of its own). He lowers his head and scuffs a back foot on the grass. He'll butt you all the way back to Maintown if you don't do something!

I'll tell him to clear off and get on with my quest. Turn to page 70.

Goats are scary – I'm running away to the Desert of Bones. Turn to page 63.

"HELP!" you shout at the top of your lungs, as you bounce along on your raft.

But what you don't realise is the ears of a mule are highly sensitive. They're *so* sensitive in fact that if you stand in the middle of London and talk to a mule in New York, she will hear what you're saying and most likely release a little wind in response. So when you bellow the word, "HELP!" right next to Tumbleweed's ear, she almost jumps out of her skin and immediately comes up with a plan to shut you up.

The old mule snatches a jawful hay from the saddlebag. She shoves it into your mouth, where it blocks your noise-hole like a big ball of hair down a gargling drain and the rocking of the water makes you swallow it whole.

GULP!

A gurgling, rumbling, grumbling sound grows inside your tummy, and then...

PAAARRRRRRRRRRRRRRRRP!

The wind hits the water like a typhoon and propels the raft back upstream, through the rapids, between the trees of Green Woodland, past the fork in the river and along the side of the desert, before finally coming to a stand-still directly opposite Crabbity Jack's Shack.

It looks like Tumbleweed isn't the only one who gets windy from eating hay.

Hurriedly, you climb off the raft to help your mule onto the bank. You see the fence encircling the small patch of farmland. The sign reads, CRABBITY JACK'S FARM - BEWARE OF THE DOGS and there's a man in the distance wearing a big straw hat. He's collecting eggs from a chicken coop. He must be Crabbity Jack.

"Howdy!" you call out. "I'm looking for some buffalo milk!"

But the man doesn't hear you.

What do you want to do?

To ignore the warning sign and open the gate, turn to page 80.

To throw a rock and attract the farmer's attention, turn to page 18.

Great Grandpappy Pete's Drawings of Medicinal Birds

The eggs of the Many-Eyed Goose are a good cure for the Sniffles. Just pop the eggs up the patient's nostrils and the problem will go away. If the treatment fails, the doctor should whisk the egg until light and fluffy, then cook over a medium heat for three minutes. It won't cure the Sniffles, but it will make a mighty fine omelette.

The beak of a Needle-Nosed Crow can be useful for cleaning a patient's teeth. Stand the bird on their face and let it hammer away at the plaque with its big, sharp, pointy beak. Patients don't like this method of tooth-cleaning, but if it's good enough for crocodiles, it's good enough for them.

The feather of a Four-Legged Duck can cure a patient's Itchity Fever. It is also good for the Wiggly Woos, the Squirmy Wirmies and the Wriggly Jigglies. Four-Legged Ducks are notoriously hard to find, but are mostly found in the str s of m nt

There's mud on the writing, but it seems to say 'streets of Maintown'. Yee-haw! Turn to page 77.

With a clippity-clop and a cloppity-clip, you trot through town on the back of your mule. Tumbleweed is a friendly creature, but a little timid. You want her to know she can trust you and the best way to do that is through her stomach.

Reaching down into your saddlebag, you take out a handful of hay. The mule chomps it down eagerly, and as she chews, a rumbling, grumbling, gargling sound grows in her stomach, until…

PAARRRRRRRRRRRRRRRP!

Wowsers! The Sheriff wasn't joking when he said hay makes Tumbleweed windy! The mule's bottom sends the pair of you shooting up into the sky like a big, hairy firework, where you gaze out at the vast Wilderness surrounding your town. It's a desolate land roamed by robbers and bandits (and goats), which is why you've never ventured out of Maintown before.

Which way will you enter the Wilderness when you come back to earth? Take a look at Great Grandpappy Pete's map in the back of this book to decide.

To travel north, turn to page 33.
To travel south, turn to page 15.

"Quick, Tumbleweed, scarper!" you shout, and the mule runs past the shepherd to continue up Purple Mountain.

The higher you go, the thinner the air. It's difficult to breathe at such a great height, so you stop for a rest in the shade of a tree. Your head is spinning, your eyelids are heavy, and suddenly the world goes black...

When you wake up, you're lying on the floor of Lightning Bolt's stable with the Sheriff by your side.

"Howdy," he smiles, softly.

"What happened?" you ask.

"You spent too long on the top of Purple Mountain and fainted," the Sheriff explains. "But Tumbleweed carried you home. I reckon you've got a real pal for life there, kid."

Gee, StoryQuester, those sure are tough beans to swallow – but with a friend like Tumbleweed, you're sure to complete the Sheriff's challenge once you're feeling better.

Go back to the start of the book to try again, or turn to page 64 to make different choice.

There's no time to waste at the store, so you run into the stable and grab a mucking-out bucket. You pour in the buffalo milk, squeeze the juice out of the dragon fruit and drop in the Four-Legged Duck feather.

At once, something wonderful happens. Little multicoloured bubbles rise to the surface of the mixture. They float up out of the bucket and then burst into tiny rainbows, each one falling back into the medicine like blossom as the feather crumbles into a sparkling, golden dust.

Your Itchity Fever medicine is ready!

Quickly, you run outside to the paddock with your bucket. The Sheriff's horse is itching himself on a tree, but with a little encouragement you persuade him to taste the mixture. He likes it. In fact, he likes it *so* much that he drinks the whole bucketful and burps out the biggest rainbow you've ever seen.

BAAAAAAAAAAAAAARP!

A beautiful arc of colours stretches out across the Wild West and the Sheriff's horse immediately stops wriggling.

You've cured Lightning Bolt of his Itchity Fever and are the most magnificent StoryQuester that ever lived! But will you tell the Sheriff *before the rodeo*, or surprise him at the barrel-race?

To go to the Sheriff's house, turn to page 82.
To take Lightning Bolt straight to the rodeo and surprise him, turn to page 36.

As you trek on towards Ancient Annie's Buffalo Farm, the blazing sun shines white in the cloudless sky. The heat is intense. Poor Tumbleweed is walking slower, and slower, but suddenly she turns tail and dashes towards Grey Rock.

Its shadow offers her a cool shade to lie down in and she won't leave until the sun drops below the horizon.

Oh, pants! Your mule has overheated and you can't carry on with your quest. Keep cool on your next attempt if you want to find that buffalo milk, partner.

Go back to the start of the book to try again, or turn to page 14 to make a different choice.

You take off your shoes and sit on the bank, hoping no alligators are lurking in the depths of Blue River.

Brrr! The water's freezing despite the warmth of the sun, but as you lower yourself in you discover the river is much shallower than it looks – the water stops at your knees! Phew!

You lead Tumbleweed into the river and wade across to the other side, where you read the sign on the wonky gate:

CRABBITY JACK'S SHACK - BEWARE OF THE DOGS

You can't see any dogs, but you *can* see an old man collecting eggs from a chicken coop. He must be Crabbity Jack.

"Howdy!" you call out. "I'm looking for some buffalo milk!"

But the man doesn't hear you. What do you want to do?

To ignore the warning sign and open the gate, turn to page 80.

To throw a rock and attract Crabbity Jack's attention, turn to page 18.

You lean forward in your saddle to feed Tumbleweed a handful of hay.

CHOMP, CHOMP, CHOMP…

The jackal lowers its head. You'll never outrun it, there's no point in trying, so you close your eyes, hold onto your breath and prepare for the worst, when…

PAARRRRRRRRRRRRRRRP!

A big gust of wind shoots out of the mule. It sends you both flying across the desert like a giant deflating balloon, leaving the jackal in a cloud of sand.

Yee-haw!

Good old Tumbleweed!

You come to a standstill near a big patch of cactus plants. There's a little pool a short distance away, with a flat rock to sit on and a tree with green coconuts. You know it's a mirage and it isn't really there. So why do you feel drawn to it like a cowboy to a new pair of pointy-toed boots with frills down the sides?

To go to the mirage, turn to page 58.
To investigate the cactus patch, turn to page 60.

55

Washing is for wimps, so you stay smelly and carry on with your challenge. After all, it's only you and the mule on this quest, and you don't suppose Tumbleweed will mind you being a bit whiffy.

You decide to search for the dragon fruit next, but you have no idea where to find one. You'll have to choose a direction and hope for the best. Go south to climb Purple Mountain, or west to explore the Desert of Bones.

The choice is yours, mighty StoryQuester!

Let's climb Purple Mountain! Turn to page 20.
The Desert of Bones sounds good! Turn to page 30.

You throw Tumbleweed at the bank so she doesn't fall into the water, and, well, it's a nice idea, but Tumbleweed is a mule. A very big, very heavy mule. Plus, you're standing on a raft in the middle of a river. It would be hard to lift an eyebrow out here, let alone a mule.

And so, as your attempt at throwing a mule fails, Tumbleweed plummets into the raging water like a big, hairy boulder.

"TUMBLEWEEEEEEEEEEEEED!" you cry.

Luckily, Blue River isn't as deep as it looks. The water barely covers Tumbleweed's knees, so she wades to safety as you and your raft drift further downstream. She will have wandered off by the time you get back to her, so your StoryQuest is over. Maybe try throwing something smaller next time, like a squirrel.

Go back to the start of the book to try again, or turn to page 7 to make a different choice. Also, please don't *actually* throw squirrels – they'll go nuts.

You tie Tumbleweed to a cactus and walk to the mirage. The pool looks so real you can see your reflection in it and a gentle breeze ripples the surface. But when you dip your hand in the clear water, something incredible happens.

Suddenly, the ground next to you swirls into a deep whirlpool and a pillar of sand grows out of the hole. It towers over you, spinning in a blur of orange, before forming the shape of a woman.

She blinks down at you through pearly eyes.

"You have *got* to be kidding me," she snorts. "Not *another* desert. Which one is it this time?"

"The, erm, Desert of Bones," you reply, timidly.

"What a cheery little name," says the woman. "Oh well, seeing as you've kindly summoned me into this *snake-pit* by sticking your hand in that imaginary pool, I suppose I should do my big intro." The sand-woman clears her throat. "BEHOLD, I AM QUEEN SANDRA, IMMORTAL RULER OF SAND!"

"Ruler of…*sand?*" you say, trying not to laugh.

"Yes, you know, those little grains of eroded rocks that get stuck in uncomfortable places when you go to the beach. Not that I'd know. No-one ever summons me to a beach. I don't suppose people need the help of an immortal being when they're sunning themselves in Barbados. No, it's all deserts and egg-timers for me. Anyway, what sand-related problem can I help with today?"

"Oh, well, I'm on a quest to—"

"Say no more," says the woman. "I might've known there was a quest involved. You'd better take this."

A golden star materialises in her hand. The sunlight catches it and the number 42 glistens on one side.

"A StoryQuest Star!" you cry. "Wow, thank you!"

"No time for all that," she replies. "Just listen up so I can leave this litter-tray and get back to my immortal plain. You must memorise the number on the StoryQuest Star, then visit the Sheriff *before the rodeo*. When you hand him the star, you'll unlock the ultimate end to your story. Oh, and do me a favour – next time you go on a quest, do it in Hawaii," and as you tuck the star safely into your pocket, Queen Sandra crumbles back into the desert and the mirage disappears.

Congratulations – you've found the StoryQuest Star!
Turn to page 60 to go back to the cactus patch and
continue your quest.

The cactus patch is full of, well, cactus plants. In fact, there are more types of cactus here than you even knew existed. There are thin ones, fat ones, tall ones, short ones, ones with flowers, ones with hair, and one that looks like Mrs Bullwinkle from the Maintown Store.

If you'd like to learn more about cactus plants, you should check out Great Grandpappy Pete's notebook.

I love cactus plants – let's read the notebook. Turn to page 38.
I couldn't care less about cactus plants – let's not.
Turn to page 35.

"I'm sorry," you say, "that's not true at all. I thought four gold coins was an unfair price to pay for a feather, so I lied," and you hang your head in shame.

But to your surprise, the shepherd holds out the feather.

"Here," he says. "It takes courage to admit you've done wrong, kid, so I reckon you deserve this free of charge."

You're speechless. Honesty really *is* the best policy! Yee-haw! And now you have your final ingredient, all that's left to do is get back to Maintown in time for the rodeo.

Thanking the shepherd, you search for your town on the landscape below. But you can't see it. You must be on the wrong side of Purple Mountain. How will you find your way home?

To climb higher up Purple Mountain for a better view of the land, turn to page 8.
To ask Tumbleweed to find the way home, turn to page 66.

You show Tumbleweed out of the Wilderness Store then go back inside to ask the storekeeper for a pint of buffalo milk.

She places a bottle of yellow gunk on the counter.

It has a whiff of public toilets about it.

"Are you sure this buffalo milk's fresh?" you ask.

"Sure is," she says. "It was fresh from the udder the day I got it. And that was only four months ago."

Four months?! In years to come, scientists will discover new life-forms in that bottle and use them to cure the most awful diseases. But for now, it's just a pint of gone-off milk.

Politely, you tell the storekeeper you've changed your mind and leave. But when you step outside, you realise something terrible has happened – Tumbleweed has gone! You see, mules have a habit of wandering off, so you can't leave them alone without securing them to a tree or a post. But don't worry, StoryQuester – you can use what you've learnt about mules to save the Sheriff's horse on your next attempt.

Go back to the start of the book to try again, or turn to page 105 to make a different choice.

You and your mule make a dash for safety as the creature starts to attack. You run and you run, and you don't look back, until finally reaching the hot sandy plains of the desert.

Phew! It looks like you lost him!

The Desert of Bones is an eerie place, littered with skeletons and skulls. From the corner of your eye, you see a wolf-like creature stalking across the sand. It's a jackal, a very hungry jackal, and its eyes are fixed upon *you*. The Wild West is crawling with dangerous animals, but jackals are a particularly cunning species. You'll have to think fast if you want to outwit this wily predator.

What's the plan, partner?

To pretend you're a mountain lion and scare the jackal away, turn to page 22.
To feed Tumbleweed some hay to calm her nerves, turn to page 55.

You cross the river and head east onto the rocky slopes of Purple Mountain. From halfway up, you see a huge flock of birds swarming above you. Some have big wings, some have little wings, some have long legs, some have short legs, some have beaks, some don't have beaks (no, wait, those are squirrels) and they're all cawing and crowing and squawking their heads off.

Suddenly, you meet a man herding sheep.

"Howdy," you say. The shepherd doffs his hat. "I'm on a quest to cure the Sheriff's horse and I'm looking for a special feather. Do you know where I might find a Four-Legged Duck?"

"Haw, haw, haw!" laughs the shepherd. "You'll be lucky, kiddo. No-one's seen a Four-Legged Duck around here for ages. Although…" From the rim of his hat, he takes a feather. It has black and white stripes with a long, pointed tip. "I did find *this* a few years back."

"Crikey!" you gasp. "Is it—"

"Yup, that's the tail feather of a Four-Legged Duck all right."

"How do you know?"

"Listen, partner, I've lived and worked on these slopes for forty-five years. Heck, I even got married on 'em once. I know every feather of every bird and this one came from a Four-Legged Duck. You can have it for a price. Have you got any gold?"

Is this guy for real? Does he *actually* have the tail feather of a Four-Legged Duck, or is he just after your money?

I think he's a bandit in disguise – let's scarper! Turn to page 50.

I'll read Great Grandpappy Pete's notebook to see if the feather is genuine. Turn to page 11.

You lean forward to whisper in Tumbleweed's ear.

"Listen," you say, "I know you're a mule and all that, but if you understand what I'm saying, please could you take me back to Maintown?"

The mule's ears twitch. Then she scuffs the ground with her hoof. Did she understand what you said? Or has she got wind again? And then…

WHOOSH!

That's not wind! *That* is the sound of a mule who's never been asked anything so politely in her whole entire life, speeding down the side of a mountain like a champion racehorse. You see, Tumbleweed knows *exactly* how to get home. She's a mule, and mules have an excellent sense of direction. She's basically a big, hairy compass on legs.

Before long, you're galloping past Crabbity Jack's Shack, across Blue River, through the Desert of Bones and into the Wilderness, where a small town appears in the distance.

Maintown!

Yee-haw!

It looks like the rodeo is about to start. Banners and flags have been strewn between the buildings, and the streets are lined with cowgirls and boys from all over the Wild West. And on the outskirts of town, a lady is charging visitors a fee to get in.

"Howdy," she smiles, as you climb out of your saddle. "Welcome to the Maintown Rodeo. That'll be three gold coins, please," and she holds out her hand for your payment.

Phew! It's lucky you didn't give all your money to that swindling shepherd!

Hurriedly, you hand over the coins and ride to the Sheriff's stables. Lightning Bolt is still scratching himself on a fencepost in the paddock. You're running out of time – you'd better make the medicine and fast.

But what will you mix the ingredients in?

To use a mucking-out bucket from the stable, turn to page 51.
To buy a bowl from Mrs Bullwinkle at the Maintown Store, turn to page 12.

"I'm sorry," you tell Crabbity Jack, "but I can't give you that money. It belongs to the Sheriff of Maintown."

"THE FERRET OF BRAINTOWN?" scowls the old man. "WHAT'RE YOU TALKIN' ABOUT? LOOK, KID, WHEN FOLK DAMAGE OTHER PEOPLE'S PROPERTY, THEY PAY TO MEND IT AND THAT'S THE RULE."

"I can pay you tomorrow," you tell him, "with my own money. I don't want to break the rule, but—"

"TAKE THE MULE?"

"No, that's not what I said. I said, I don't want to *break the rule.*"

"I SUPPOSE I *COULD* TAKE THE MULE INSTEAD OF A PAYMENT."

"That's not what I said! I said, *break the rule, BREAK THE RULE!*"

"ALL RIGHT, ALL RIGHT, NO NEED TO KEEP GOING ON ABOUT IT!" Crabbity Jack takes hold of Tumbleweed's reins and leads her onto his farm. "THERE, I'VE TAKEN THE MULE. NOW GET OFF MY LAND, YOU LITTLE VANDAL, AND DON'T COME BACK!"

You've lost your mule to Crabbity Jack, but you

were *so* close to finding that buffalo milk. Good luck on your next attempt, StoryQuester!

Go back to the start of the book to try again, or turn to page 18 to make a different choice.

"Hey, goat!" you shout, climbing down from your mule. "I'm not scared of you and your spinning eyeball! Leave us alone, or I'll...I'll...I'll shoo you away!"

The goat doesn't care. In fact, he looks even angrier now than he did before.

"MEEHHHHHHHH!"

"Right, that's it," you say. "Here it comes. *SHOO!*"

Your voice is like a red flag to a bull. The goat lowers his horns, snorts fiercely then charges towards you, butting you so hard you soar into the air and land on the very top of Purple Mountain.

Gee, the goats of the Wild West sure are strong!

You look down from your lofty perch. Tumbleweed is already making her way back to Maintown and you wish you were going with her. But the rocks here are too steep to climb, so you stay on the summit all night, listening to the taunting cries of the goats pushing up through the darkness below.

"MEEHHHHHHHH!"

Go back to the start of the book to try again, or turn to page 45 to make a different choice.

You approach the hermit to ask about Four-Legged Ducks.

"Excuse me, sir. I'm sorry to bother you, but—"

"I know what you're thinking," the man interrupts. He has a posh British accent and a piece of grass stuck between his two front teeth. "You're wondering where you know me from, aren't you?" (You're not. You thought he was a hermit.) "It's me! Horatio Smythe, famous scientist and all-round good egg." (He doesn't look like a scientist. Or an egg.) "My colleague and I, Professor Rogers, have been living here in Green Woodland for the last two years. We're studying the wildlife. The Professor just popped out to investigate some Silver-Feathered Goose chicks down on the lake. Would you like my autograph?"

"Erm, that's okay," you reply. "I just wondered if you've seen any Four-Legged Ducks?"

"Four-Legged Ducks, eh?" muses Horatio Smythe. "Those are mountain birds – you won't find any down here. Are you sure you don't want my autograph? I could sign your mule."

You can't tell if Horatio Smythe really is a scientist, or if he's a wagon-wheel short of a stagecoach. So as the scruffy man searches his tent for a pen, you decide

71

to check Great Grandpappy Pete's notebook to see if he's right about Four-Legged Ducks.

Quickly, you take the item out of your saddlebag and flick through the pages. But in your hurry, the book slips through your fingers and falls onto the muddy ground.

Oh, dear. Some of the pages are dirty and smudged. Do you still want to check Great Grandpappy Pete's notes, or will you trust Horatio Smythe and go straight to Purple Mountain?

To trust Horatio Smythe and go straight to Purple Mountain, turn to page 64.
To check Great Grandpappy Pete's muddy notes, turn to page 48.

You've had enough poo-shovelling to last you a lifetime, so you offer to shear Crabbity Jack's sheep instead.

His flock are grazing uphill from the shack. It's windy on this side of the building and as you walk towards the field a sudden breeze blows a spattering of grit into your eyes.

Ouch!

It stings like salt and you can't blink it out. But there's a job to be done, so you carefully take hold of the nearest sheep and start shearing. A pile of wool forms on the grass, then Crabbity Jack comes out of his shack to inspect your handiwork. He's carrying a bottle of buffalo milk and he looks pleased with your sheep-shearing efforts.

Until suddenly, he stops.

He squints across the field.

His nostrils flare like a cowboy's jeans and his jaw drops to his chest.

"*ROVER!*" he cries. "*MY DEAR ROVER!*"

Rover? That's a weird name for a sheep.

With a hard blink, the grit finally leaves your eyes, your vision clears and…

Argh! That's not a sheep! It's a dog! It's a bald dog

standing next to a big pile of hair! You've accidentally shaved Crabbity Jack's dog and you can't make a jumper out of dog hair! Well, you probably *could* but you definitely shouldn't.

What are you going to do?

To offer Crabbity Jack some money, turn to page 97.
To grab the milk and leg-it, turn to page 79.

Great Grandpappy Pete's Drawings of Medicinal Feathers

The feather of a long-Nosed Peacock is good for patients who are being sat on by a horse. A doctor should use the feather to tickle the animal under its armpit or on the foot. This will make the horse giggle so much it will fall off the patient. Please note, finding the armpit of an animal without arms can often prove tricky.

The feather of a Sabre-Toothed Robin is an excellent treatment for patients who are stuck in the swing-door of a saloon. The medically trained person should drop the feather near the patient, shouting, "Argh! A Sabre-Toothed Robin! We're all goners!" and the patient will immediately unstick themselves from the door and run off down the street.

The feather of a Four-legged Duck is known for its use on patients who prickle themselves on a cactus. It can be mixed with a pint of buffalo milk and the juice of a fresh dragon fruit and used as an effective cure for Itchity Fever.

Yee-haw! You've learnt that a Four-Legged Duck's feather is stripy! Turn to page 103 to continue with your quest.

You continue your lion impression by showing your teeth and snarling fiercely.

"RARGH!"

The real mountain lion looks at you with interest. He pads towards you. Then he sniffs your face and his eyes soften. He thinks you're his long-lost cub, the same cub who wandered into the Wilderness one day and never returned. He hasn't seen you for years, but now you're back and soon to be reunited with the pride.

Ah, it's a Wild West *miracle.*

Of course, it's actually no miracle at all. You're just *really* good at animal impressions. But you can't argue with a mountain lion, so you follow him to Purple Mountain where you change your name to Rory and live as one of the pride for the rest of your days. It's not a bad life, here in the den. But the vegetarian options are limited.

Go back to the start of the book to try again, or turn to page 22 to make a different choice.

Great Grandpappy Pete says you can find a Four-Legged Duck on the streets of Maintown, so you thank Horatio Smythe for his help (even though he was no help at all) and steer Tumbleweed towards Blue River. From there, you go through the desert, across the Wilderness and back to Maintown, where the rodeo preparations are well underway.

Banners and flags have been hung between buildings, people are practising their horse-riding skills and there are tables full of delicious snacks outside the local saloon. And amongst it all, the Sheriff is pacing the street with worry.

"Howdy, partner!" he cries, as he sees you enter the town. "Have you found everythin' we need for Lightnin' Bolt's medicine?"

"Almost," you reply. "I have the buffalo milk and a fresh dragon fruit. And according to Great Grandpappy Pete's notebook, I can find a Four-Legged Duck right here on the streets of Maintown."

The Sheriff frowns.

"Really?" he says. "I've lived in Maintown my whole life and I ain't never seen no Four-Legged Ducks. Gimme a look at those notes, kid."

You hand the Sheriff his grandfather's book.

"The page is muddy," he says, "but I'm pretty sure that says Four-Legged Ducks can be found in the *streams of mountains.*'"

"Oh, no!" you cry. "You're right, and so was Horatio Smythe! Four-Legged ducks really *do* live on Purple Mountain!"

"Horatio Smythe?" frowns the Sheriff. "You mean the world famous scientist and all round good-egg? Did you get his autograph?"

The rodeo is about to begin and you don't have time to go back out of town. But well done for finding two ingredients, partner! Yee-haw!

Go back to the start of the book to try again, or turn to page 71 to make a different choice.

You grab the bottle of milk from Crabbity Jack and run towards the gate. It's a bad idea. For a start, thieves never prosper. And for another, Crabbity Jack might be old, but, wow, is he fast.

The aging farmer chases after you like an angry bull, shouting naughty words and swinging a spade over his head. You panic and speed up your pace, catching a foot on the uneven ground in your hurry and – whoosh! – up you go, soaring into the air like an arrow, over the sheep, past the buffalo and straight through the roof of a small chicken coop.

KERASH!

Crabbity Jack comes storming across the field.

"YOU THIEVIN' SCOUNDREL!" yells the farmer. "I'M TAKIN' YOUR MULE AS PAYMENT FOR THAT BUFFALO MILK, NOT TO MENTION THOSE EGGS YOU'VE BROKEN! NOW GET OFF MY LAND BEFORE I THROW YOU OFF!"

Go back to the start of the book to try again, or turn to page 73 to make a different choice.

You ignore the sign saying, CRABBITY JACK'S SHACK – BEWARE OF THE DOGS and open the gate.

The rusty hinge creaks as you step onto Crabbity Jack's land. It acts as an alarm and a huge pack of dogs immediately bursts out of the shack.

"WOOF! WOOF! WOOF! WOOF! WOOF!"

There are at least thirty of them, maybe more, and they're running towards you on thundering paws like one big, hairy monster. Before you know it they've knocked you over and pinned you down on the grass.

But they're not snarling or growling, they're not biting or snapping. And then you realise – these aren't guard-dogs, they're a big happy family of Golden Retrievers.

You laugh at the dogs' funny open-mouthed smiles, as they dance around with their tongues hanging out, wagging their tails and licking you on the face. Crabbity Jack hears the commotion. He spins around and glares at you through a monobrow the size of a young sheep. He has a face like a leather saddlebag and ears like two rashers of crispy bacon.

"WHAT'S ALL THE NOISE?" he shouts. Then he marches over and stares down at you. "WHO ARE YOU AND WHADDA YOU WANT?"

"Sorry to disturb you, sir," you say, jumping to your feet. "I'm on a quest to cure the Sheriff's horse and I'm looking for a pint of buffalo milk."

Crabbity Jack's rubbery forehead folds into his hat like a concertina.

"BUNGALOW SILK? WHAT'S THAT?"

"No, I said, *buffalo milk*."

"DOMINO STILTS?"

"No, *buffalo milk*."

"A TOMATO KILT?"

It seems Crabbity Jack is a little hard of hearing.

"No, sir, I'm looking for some *buffalo milk*."

"OH, BUFFALO MILK!" he replies. "WHY DIDN'T YOU SAY SO? I GOT PLENTY – IF YOU LEND A HAND ON MY FARM, I'LL FETCH YOU A PINT. YOU CAN EITHER SHEAR A FEW SHEEP, OR SHOVEL SOME BUFFALO DUNG. WHICH IS IT TO BE?"

Pass me the shovel! Turn to page 40.
I'd rather try my hand at sheep-shearing. Turn to page 73.

You trot to the Sheriff's house to tell him you've cured Lightning Bolt of his Itchity Fever.

"Well, bless my boots!" he exclaims. "That sure is the finest darn thing I ever did hear. You should be mighty proud of yourself, partner! I'd love to hear all about your Wild West adventures, but first things first – do you have the StoryQuest Star for me?"

If you collected the StoryQuest Star from Queen Sandra, turn to the page number you saw glittering on the object when she handed it over.
If you don't have the star, don't worry, you're still awesome! Turn to page 100.

"Of course I'm telling the truth," you reply. "Do you think I'd lie about a poor, sick little puppy?"

The shepherd puts the Four-Legged Duck Feather back into the rim of his hat.

"You can't pull the wool over a shepherd's eyes," he says. "I can tell when folk are lying. You keep your coins, and I'll keep my feather. Good luck with your quest, kid," and with that, he ushers his flock to the other side of the mountain.

Oh, dear. The shepherd has seen right through you and you have to start your feather-hunt all over again. But after searching the rocky slopes of Purple Mountain for the next three hours, when darkness falls you're forced to head back to Maintown without your final ingredient.

Go back to the start of the book to try again, or turn to page 85 to make a different choice.

You pick up an animal bone and part the leaves of the prickly plant. Then you reach through, take hold of the dragon fruit and with a gentle snap it leaves the cactus.

Congratulations!

You've collected your second ingredient!

Yee-haw!

All you need now is the feather of a Four-Legged Duck and your quest is complete.

But you won't find any ducks here in the desert, it's far too dry. The Sheriff's divination stick could show you where to find water, or you could try looking in the babbling streams of Purple Mountain.

Which would you like to do?

To look on Purple Mountain, turn to page 64.

To use the divination stick, turn to page 5.

You decide to make up a sob-story, one that's sad enough to convince the shepherd to part with his feather for a better price.

"I can't give you all four of my coins," you tell him, "because I need the rest to buy food for my poor, sick little puppy."

Everyone loves a puppy, right?

"Well, I wouldn't want a sick puppy to go hungry," the shepherd replies. "Okay, if you swear you're telling the truth, you can buy the feather for one gold coin."

Well, this is yee-h*awkward*. Are you going to tell the truth, or carry on with your lie?

To reply, "Of course I'm telling the truth," turn to page 83.
To own-up and admit it's a lie, turn to page 61.

You lean forward to whisper in Tumbleweed's ear.

"Listen," you say, "I know you're a mule and all that, but if you understand what I'm saying, please could you take me back to Maintown?"

The mule's ears twitch. She scuffs the ground with her hoof. Did she understand what you said? Or has she got wind again? And then…

WHOOSH!

That's not wind. *That* is the sound of a mule who's never been asked to do anything so politely in her whole entire life, speeding down the side of a mountain like a champion racehorse. You see, Tumbleweed knows *exactly* how to get home. She's a mule, and mules have an excellent sense of direction. She's basically a big, hairy compass on legs.

Before long, you're galloping past Crabbity Jack's Shack, across Blue River, through the desert and into the Wilderness, where a small town appears in the distance.

Maintown! Yee-haw!

It looks like the rodeo is about to start. Banners and flags have been strewn between the buildings, and the streets are lined with cowgirls and boys from all over the Wild West. And on the outskirts of town, a lady is charging visitors a fee to get in.

"Howdy," she smiles. "Welcome to the Maintown Rodeo. That'll be three gold coins, please," and she holds out her hand for your payment.

Dagnabbit! You don't have any coins. You gave them all to the shepherd on Purple Mountain. But what you *do* have is a plan.

Quickly, you take out the buffalo milk, the dragon fruit and the Four-Legged Duck feather.

"I can't pay to get into Maintown," you tell the woman, "but the Sheriff urgently needs these ingredients. Can you make sure he gets them, please?"

The woman snorts.

"Does this *look* like a delivery service?" she asks. "If you ain't got no money, kid, just clear off."

You thought this might happen, it's all part of the plan, so you feed Tumbleweed the tiniest piece of hay and…

PARP.

The woman scowls. Her face turns green. Then her eyes bulge and her nose wiggles.

"All right, all right!" she cries. "I'll make sure the Sheriff gets the ingredients! Just take your windy mule and get outta here before everyone leaves town!"

Good old Tumbleweed has saved the day!

And later that evening, once the rodeo has

finished, you return to Maintown to walk your mule back to her shed. The Sheriff is still clearing up outside the ol' saloon.

"*There* you are!" he exclaims. "I was wonderin' where you'd got to. Thanks for sendin' me those ingredients, partner – you sure are the best stablehand a Sheriff could wish for. I mixed the medicine in time for the barrel-race and Lightnin' Bolt won first prize. But we ain't the ones who did all the hard work, so I reckon it's *you* who deserves this."

He hands you a big golden trophy.

"Wow!" you smile. "Thanks, Sheriff! But I couldn't have done it without Tumbleweed."

The man's moustache gives an impish twitch.

"Sure thing," he replies. "Which is why I've put some extra hay in her shed tonight," and as the blazing sun sinks into the distant horizon, a very happy, very windy mule zips across the skyline like a hairy shooting-star.

Yee-haw!

Congratulations! You've completed the challenge and cured the Sheriff's horse!
If you want to find the ultimate ending, go back to the start of the book and try again.

A wash in Blue River is just what you need and it certainly makes you smell better.

But when you climb out of the water, you're followed by a long, green alligator. Two pointed teeth hang over its bottom lip and its huge tail lashes the ground like a whip as it stalks towards you.

Uh oh. The alligators of the Wild West are almost as dangerous as the goats. You'd better get out of here fast. Where will you run to?

To head for Purple Mountain, turn to page 45.
To go to the Desert of Bones, turn to page 63.

You shelter from the sun in the disused gold mine. It's much cooler in here and Tumbleweed is glad of the shade. But suddenly, there's a noise in the darkness. A man wearing scruffy clothes walks in from an adjoining room.

"Howdy," he says. "What're you doing in Dead Man's Gorge?"

"I'm on a quest to cure the Sheriff's horse," you reply. "Do you work here?"

"Sure do," says the man. "The name's Stanley Miner. I've worked here for more than eighty years and I've only been dead for twelve of 'em."

GASP!

"You mean you're a g-g-g-ghost?"

"That's right," he says. "But there ain't no need for all that stuttering. Folk weren't scared of me when I was alive, so they shouldn't be scared of me now. This is my gorge, partner, and you'll always be welcome here."

Two animal ghosts materialise through the far wall. One is a horse and the other's a donkey. Tumbleweed looks curiously at the pair. Then she trots over and the three of them rub noses.

"Well, blow me down with a stick of dynamite,"

90

breathes Stanley Miner. "Tumbleweed, is that you?"

The mule releases a little wind.

PARP.

"It *is* you!" cries the ghost. He floats over to join the animals. "These two are Tumbleweed's parents," he explains. "They were working in the mine when she was born, but the Sheriff of Maintown rescued her when she was a foal. He gave her a much better life than she woulda had here." Stanley Miner strokes Tumbleweed's head like a long-lost relative. "How's life treating you, old pal?"

Tumbleweed is so happy to see her family again you don't have the heart to leave. So you stay in the disused gold mine for the rest of the day and don't go back to Maintown until sunfall.

Good for you, partner – some things are more important than winning a rodeo. You haven't completed the quest, but you're an excellent human being.

Go back to the start of the book to try again, or turn to page 14 to make a different choice.

When you enter Snake Valley, you're surprised to find no snakes at all. It's just a big valley full of rocks.

"This place should be called *Rock* Valley," you chuckle, as Ancient Annie's Buffalo Farm appears in the distance. "Whoever named this place needs their eyes tested. There's not a single snake in the whole—"

HISSSSSSSSSSSSSSSSSSSSSSSS!

The rocks move. A snake slithers out from each of them. They've been waiting for you to reach the middle of the valley and now you're surrounded. Tumbleweed is terrified. In fact, the poor mule is *so* scared she releases a little wind.

PARP.

Whoa, that smells worse than the Sheriff's boots!

Your eyes water, your nose runs, your face turns green. But somehow you manage to keep hold of Tumbleweed's reins until the air clears.

Blinking the tears from your eyes, you realise the snakes are still there. But they're lying on their backs with their tongues hanging out. Tumbleweed's whiffy wind has knocked them all senseless.

Yee-haw!

Quickly, you gallop to the other side of Snake Valley to escape the serpents and see a small wooden building near a field full of buffalo. An old woman is digging potatoes. When she sees you approaching, she throws her trowel onto the soil and runs towards you.

"Bless my buffalo!" she cries, pulling you out of your saddle and flinging her arms around your neck. It's meant to be a hug, but it feels more like a wrestling contest. "You're the first person I've seen in years! *Years!* No-one ever dares go around Grey Rock to visit Ancient Annie! Oh gee, I sure am pleased to see you!"

The old woman has quite a grip.

"I…can't…breathe," you tell her.

"Sorry," she says, releasing your neck. "Now, what can I do for you, kid?"

"I'm on a quest to cure the Sheriff's horse," you tell her. "I'm looking for some buffalo milk. Do you have any?"

"Of course," she replies, "anything for my new friend. But first, won't you come in for a cup of tea and a chat? Did I mention it's been years since I've seen anyone?"

To go inside for a cup of tea, turn to page 29.
To politely refuse and get on with your quest, turn to page 26.

You make a dash for the cactus patch on the back of your trusty mule and with a roar the lion gives chase. He's closing in on Tumbleweed's tail, despite your speedy head-start, and as you skid between the cacti he lifts his enormous paws and pounces.

"MEEYOWCH!"

Silly lion. He wasn't looking where he was going and now he's scratched himself on one of the plants. You feel a bit sorry for him, but you're also glad he's running across the desert with his tail between his legs.

That was a close call, partner!

Breathing a sigh of relief, you gaze around at the plants. Who knew there were so many types of cactus? Some have needles like thorns, some have prickles like hairs, some have beautiful flowers like giant butterflies, and one of them looks a bit like Mrs Bullwinkle from the Maintown Store.

You can learn more about cactus plants in Great Grandpappy Pete's notebook. Would you like to take a look?

Yes, please, I love cactus plants. Turn to page 38.

No, thanks. I really couldn't care less about cactus plants. Turn to page 35.

Climbing out of your saddle, you peer down at the mega-bird to find a man's face staring out of the feathers.

"At *last!*" cries the man. "I thought I'd be stuck in this mud forever!"

"Crikey," you say, "who are you? And why are you wearing those feathers on your head?"

"It's a disguise," he explains, "to fool the birds. Pull me out of here and I'll introduce myself." You do as he asks and the man takes off his disguise. "The name's Rogers. Professor Rogers. I've been camping in Green Woodland with that pompous idiot of a scientist, Horatio Smythe. We're here to study the wildlife."

"Horatio Smythe? You mean that hermit I bumped into earlier on?"

"He's no hermit," says Professor Rogers. "Horatio Smythe is the Queen of England's third cousin twice removed and he's incredibly self-absorbed. Last Friday, I left our tent to study a flock of Silver-Feathered Goose chicks. I've been stuck in that mud ever since and I bet Horatio hasn't even noticed I'm missing."

"You've been out here for *five days?*" you gasp.

"You must be starving."

"Ravenous," nods the professor. He points at the mule. "Is that a dragon fruit sticking out of your saddlebag?"

"Oh, yes, it is, but—"

Before you can stop him, the professor snatches the fruit and shoves it into his mouth, skin and all. You watch in horror as the last dribble of it runs down his chin.

"Delicious!" he smiles. "Thanks so much, old fellow. Tell you what, let's ditch that self-important scientist and I'll treat you to a slap-up meal at the Maintown saloon."

Cripes! Professor Rogers has eaten one of your ingredients. You don't have time to go back to the cactus patch for another dragon fruit. Plus, none of the professor' feathers came from a Four-Legged Duck. Oh well, at least you're getting a free meal after all your hard work.

Well done for finding two ingredients, heroic StoryQuester – you should be mighty pleased with yourself!

StoryQuest over. Go back to the start of the book to try again.

"I'm really sorry about your dog," you tell Crabbity Jack. "Here, take these coins and buy him a sweater. I've only got four, but you can have them all."

"LABRADOR?" scowls the old farmer, wiggling his finger in his left ear. "ROVER AIN'T NO LABRADOR. HE'S A GOLDEN RETRIEVER."

"I said, you can *have them all*," you reply. You place the gold coins in Crabbity Jack's hand. "To buy a sweater for your dog."

"YOU WANNA BUY MY DOG?"

"No, that's not what I'm saying—"

"FOUR GOLD COINS AIN'T GONNA BUY MY ROVER. BUT THROW IN THE MULE AND WE'VE GOT A DEAL."

Crabbity Jack leads Tumbleweed to the buffalo field then throws you off his land. The old mule will have lots of grass to graze on and plenty of animal friends to play with, so you shouldn't feel too sad. Plus, you have your bald dog to comfort you now.

Go back to the start of the book to try again, or turn to page 73 to make a different choice.

Tumbleweed moves slowly away from the hermit and you pass by unnoticed, still holding the divination stick in the air.

"This stick is a waste of time," you tell the mule. "We only fell into that river because I wasn't looking where I was going. I'm getting rid of it," and you throw it over your shoulder.

SPLASH!

The divination stick has landed in a small woodland stream (how does it *do* that?). The water is moving at speed and you trot alongside it until you reach a small clearing.

A gently bubbling waterfall trickles into a sparkling lake, nestled amongst the trees like a hidden diamond. There are tall reeds on the far side and a cluster of lily-pads in the middle, and there, floating and playing and messing around on the lake, are hundreds, no, *thousands* of birds!

There are red birds, green birds, fat birds, thin birds, tall birds, short birds, birds with beaks, birds without beaks (no, wait, those are frogs), and there, hiding amongst the reeds, there's a really strange-looking bird with totally mismatched feathers. It's like someone has taken a single feather from each of the other birds and sewed them together to make one giant mega-bird.

If there's a Four-Legged Duck to be found, surely *this* is the place to find it. But the birds' feet are all underwater. How will you find out if any are the species you're looking for?

If you want to check Great Grandpappy Pete's notebook for clues, turn to page 75.
If you want to take a closer look at the mega-bird, turn to page 95.

"That's okay," says the Sheriff, "you don't need the star to enjoy the rodeo. Come on, partner, let's go."

This year's celebrations are the best you've ever seen. There are people in fancy-dress, a sheep-herding contest, a ragtime band playing your favourite songs, line-dancing groups, yummy food and the most popular riding contest this side of Blue River – the grand barrel-race.

All the best riders have travelled across the Wild West to compete. They saddle-up and gallop around two barrels, in and out of the obstacles as fast as their horses will carry them, and the quickest time wins. But of course, no-one ever beats the Sheriff and his fine horse, and that's all part of the fun.

At the end of the competition, Lightning Bolt is awarded a big rosette and the Sheriff tells everyone about his incredible stablehand, who crossed deserts and climbed mountains to save his trusty stead.

A huge cheer goes up as you and Tumbleweed take your place next to the Sheriff.

"I've been thinking," he says, as the crowd go crazy, "a Wild West explorer like you shouldn't be shovelling horse poo for pocket money – how would you like to be my Deputy instead?"

"No more poo-shovelling!" you cry. "Amazing!"

And later that evening, as the reddening sun sinks into the distant horizon, you walk Tumbleweed back to her shed with your shiny new Deputy's badge.

"Gee," you tell your four-legged friend, "this sure has been a mighty fine adventure."

Tumbleweed releases a little wind, and you're pretty sure what she means by that is…

"Yee-haw!"

Congratulations! You've completed the Sheriff's challenge and you're the new Deputy Sheriff of Maintown!

If you want to find the ultimate ending to your story, go back to the start of the book and try again.

Great Grandpappy's Pete's notebook has helped you find your next ingredient. Dragon fruits grow on cactus plants and there's one right there in front of you.

Yee-haw!

But the fruit is tucked between the spiny leaves of the cactus. If you scratch yourself you could end up with Itchity Fever, just like the Sheriff's horse, so you'll have to take care when picking it.

There's a rock on the sand. You could throw it at the dragon fruit to knock it down. Or you could use an animal bone to part the prickly leaves and carefully reach in.

Which would you like to do?

To use the rock, turn to page 104.
To use the bone, turn to page 84.

After checking Great Grandpappy Pete's notebook, you realise only two birds on the lake have striped feathers.

One is a small duck hiding under a low-hanging branch. It's sat on a nest, so you can't tell how many legs it has without taking a closer look.

The other is the mega-bird. At least some of its feathers are stripy, but you're not sure if any of them are *exactly* like Great Grandpappy Pete's drawing.

Which bird is most likely to be the Four-Legged Duck?

To take a closer look at the bird on the nest, turn to page 23.

To check out the mega-bird, turn to page 95.

You pick up a rock to throw at the dragon fruit, to find a scorpion hiding underneath it. The critter is startled, his tail twitches, and...

"Youch!"

Oh, no! You've been stung!

The scorpion's sting is venomous and your hand swells up to twice its normal size. It's so painful you almost pass out. You'll need to go back to Maintown to have it checked out, but try the challenge again when you've seen the doctor.

Go back to the start of the book to try again, or turn to page 102 to make a different choice.

The Wilderness Store has a sign on the door saying NO BANDITS, RUSTLERS OR DONKEYS ALLOWED. Luckily, you're none of these things, so you climb out of your saddle and enter the building.

Rows of wooden shelves line the walls. They're covered with fresh groceries, like cabbages, cauliflowers, parsnips and carrots. A middle-aged lady in a chequered dress is standing behind the counter.

"Welcome to the Wilderness Store," she says. "What can I get for you?"

"I'm on a quest to cure the Sheriff's horse," you tell her, "and I'm looking for a pint of—"

But suddenly, Tumbleweed barges into the shop and chomps down a huge mouthful of carrots.

CHOMP!

"You can't bring a donkey in here!" cries the shopkeeper. "Didn't you see the sign?"

You're embarrassed, so you try to lighten the mood with an amusing reply.

"I saw it," you say, "but she's not a donkey – she's a mule."

The woman doesn't find you funny, and now Tumbleweed has moved onto the cabbages.

CHOMP!

"Get that mangy creature out of my store!" cries the woman. "Or go somewhere else for your shopping!"

What do you want to do?

If you're unhappy with the customer service at the Wilderness Store and want to try Crabbity Jack's Shack instead, turn to page 25.

If you appreciate the Wilderness Store's attention to health and safety, and want to put Tumbleweed outside, turn to page 62.

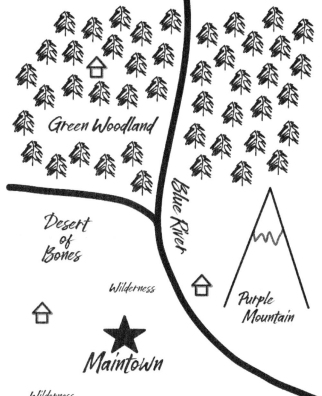

Great Grandpappy Pete's
Map of the Wild West

Green Woodland

Blue River

Desert
of
Bones

Wilderness

★
Maintown

Purple
Mountain

Wilderness

Wilderness

Snake
Valley

Grey Rock

Dead Man's
Gorge

STORYQUEST

CHOOSE THE PAGE - UNLOCK THE ADVENTURE

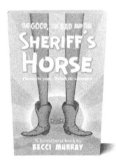

COLLECT THEM ALL!

Laugh along with Billy, as he boosts his brain
to the size of Venus in this hilariously
gruesome chapter book also by

Becci Murray

You'll find lots of very serious poems about really important stuff (like toenails, sausages and yaks) in this hilariously irreverent collection of illustrated poetry from children's author Becci Murray.

AVAILABLE NOW IN PAPERBACK OR EBOOK!

Becci Murray is a British children's author from Gloucestershire, England. She's also mum to a teenager, a chocolate labrador, a big-footed cat and a giant snail. You can learn more about Becci's books or send her a message by visiting the Llama House Children's Books website - she would love to hear from you!

WWW.LLAMAHOUSEBOOKS.COM

Printed in Great Britain
by Amazon

79943383R00068